PUSS IN BOOTS

7 장화신은 고양이

Charles Perrault

KB218530

WorldCom Edu

Adapted by **Lori Olcott**
Illustrated by **Shin Yun-Kun**

Copyright © WorldCom Edu 2003

Published in Korea in 2003 by WorldCom Edu

Printed and distributed by WorldCom Edu

작가와 작품 설명

샤를 페로(Charles Perrault)는 프랑스 파리 태생의 동화작가이다. 17세기 프랑스를 대표하는 비평가이기도 한 그는 1670년 아카데미 프랑세즈 회원이 되어 집회에서 낭독한『루이 대왕의 세기(世紀)』를 계기로 커다란 논쟁을 불러 일으키기도 했다. 그가 쓴 동화의 제재(題材)로는 후세의『그림 동화』와 공통된 것이 많으나, 현실과 상상의 세계가 절묘하게 조화되어, 그를 프랑스 아동문학의 아버지라고 부르기도 한다.

이 작품 외에도 유럽의 민담에 문학적 표현을 가미한『푸른 수염』『빨간 망토』『신데렐라』『잠자는 숲 속의 미녀』등 교훈적인 내용의 동화를 많이 썼다.

작품 설명

방앗간주인이 세상을 떠나자 막내 아들은 유산으로 고양이 한 마리만 물려받게 되나, 이 고양이의 재치로 후작이라는 지위를 얻고 공주와 결혼하게 되기까지의 과정을 그렸다. 이 작품은 C.페로의『거위 아주머니 이야기』에 실려 있는 이야기로, 젊은 사람들에게 있어서 처세술과 임기응변의 술책이 부모에게서 물려받은 재산보다 쓸모가 있다는 교훈을 들려 주고 있다.

Introduction

Hello, and thank you for your interest in Worldcom's Story House! I hope you and your children enjoy the stories and characters we present to you here.

These Fairy tales have been passed down from parent to child for generations and generations. They usually teach a lesson. They teach the values that are important in every culture; like being kind, generous and helpful to others. They show that looks can be deceiving. Something beautiful, can be cruel and evil. But something ugly, can be good and loving. They also teach the value of patience. Rewards for good deeds don't always come quickly. But be patient, and the good deeds you do will bring good deeds to you. And if you keep working hard, your efforts will pay off.

I have tried my best to re-tell these stories in modern and natural English, without being too complicated or too hard. Most middle school children can read these stories. But I hope that parents and other adults will enjoy reading these books with their children too. There are interesting parts in each story. I hope there is enough that everyone will enjoy reading the story and listening to the native speakers.

Again, thank you for joining us in Story House. We hope you enjoy your stay.

이 책을 펴내며

안녕하세요. 월드컴의 Story House에 오신 것을 환영합니다. 부디 여러분과 여러분의 자녀들이 이 책이 들려주는 이야기들을 만끽하시길 바랍니다.

이 동화들은 부모에서 아이들에게로 여러 세대에 걸쳐 전해내려 온 이야기로서 교훈을 담고 있습니다. 이웃에게 친절하고 서로 도우면서 아낌없이 베푸는 것, 이러한 가치관의 중요성을 일깨워 주죠. 이러한 것들은 때때로 반대로 표현되기도 합니다. 겉보기에는 아름답지만 잔인하고 사악할 수 있으며, 비록 흉칙하게 보여도 착하고 사랑을 베푸는 사람일 수 있다는 것입니다. 이러한 이야기들은 우리에게 인내의 가치를 일깨워 주기도 합니다. 선한 행동의 대가는 그 즉시 되돌아오지 않습니다. 그러나 참고 기다린다면, 여러분의 선한 행동은 보답을 받을 것입니다. 그리고 열심히 노력한다면 그에 상응하는 결과를 얻을 것입니다.

저는 이 이야기들을 너무 복잡하거나 어렵지 않도록 현대적이고 자연스러운 영어로 전달하기 위해 최선을 다했습니다. 이 책은 중학교 수준의 학생이라면 누구든지 읽을 수 있습니다. 그러나 부모님을 비롯한 모든 이들이 자녀분들과 함께 이 책을 즐길 수 있기를 바랍니다. 이야기마다 제각기 재미있는 부분들이 있습니다. 네이티브들이 들려주는 생생한 이야기는 현장감을 더해 주어 자신도 모르는 사이에 동화세계에 빠져들게 될 것임을 믿어 의심치 않습니다.

다시 한 번 저희 Story House에 오신 것을 감사드리며, 계속 많은 사랑 부탁드립니다.

Lori Olcott

등장인물

장화신은 고양이

한낱 고양이에 불과하지만 뛰어난 재치와 처세술로
방앗간집의 막내아들을 후작이라는 지위로까지
끌어올리는 데 커다란 공을 세운다.

셋째 아들

방앗간 주인의 막내아들로 잘생긴 외모를 갖추고 있다.
아버지가 남겨주신 유산으로 고양이를 받게 된다.

왕

한 나라의 왕이라는 고귀한 신분이면서도 다른 사람의
은혜를 잊지 않으며, 장화신은 고양이와 절친한 사이가 된다.

 마법사

 공주

 마을 사람들

Contents

SH-07-C
MP3

Chapter 1

Once there was a poor miller who only owned three things, a donkey, a cat and a mill. He could grind meal with the mill. He could carry bags of meal to the market with his donkey. But, the cat, well, he couldn't do anything with the cat except catch mice.

once 옛날에

poor miller 가난한 방앗간 주인

own 소유하다

donkey 당나귀

cat 고양이

mill 방앗간

grind meal 가루로 갈다[빻다]

carry 운반하다, 나르다

market 시장

except …을 제외하고

catch 잡다

mice (mouse의 복수형)쥐

● ● ● ● ● ● ● ● ● ● ● ● ●

Once there was a poor miller who only owned three things
a donkey, a cat and a mill.

옛날에 가진 것이라곤 오직 당나귀, 고양이, 그리고 방앗간, 이
세 가지밖에 없는 가난한 방앗간 주인이 살고 있었습니다.

He could carry bags of meal to the market with his donkey.

그는 당나귀로 곡식자루를 시장으로 나를 수가 있었습니다.

he couldn't do anything with the cat except catch mice.

고양이는 쥐잡는 것 외에는 아무것도 할 수 없었습니다.

The miller also had three sons.
The oldest son was very strong.
The second son was very smart. And,
the youngest son was only handsome.
When the old miller finally died he left
all he had to his sons.
To his oldest son he left the mill.
The oldest son worked the mill and
earned a living. The miller left his
donkey to his second son. The second
son took the donkey and set out in
search of his fortune.

also 또한, 역시
have(-had-had) 가지고 있다
son 아들
oldest 가장 나이가 많은
strong 강한, 힘센
second 두 번째의
smart 똑똑한, 영리한
youngest 가장 어린
handsome 잘생긴

some time later 얼마 후에
finally 마침내
die 죽다
leave(-left-left) 남기다
work 일하다
earn a living 생계를 유지하다
take(-took-taken) 데려가다
set(-set-set) out 떠나다
in search of fortune 성공을 찾아서

● ● ● ● ● ● ● ● ● ● ● ● ● ●

When the old miller finally died he left all he had to his sons.
마침내 그 늙은 방앗간 주인은 그가 가지고 있는 모든 것을 아들들에게
남기고는 세상을 떠났습니다.

The oldest son worked the mill and earned a living.
큰아들은 방앗간에서 일을 하며 생계를 꾸렸습니다.

But, for the youngest son there was only the cat. The youngest son was very fond of the cat, but he did not know what to do with him.

I am going to starve. I will surely die with only this cat.

Just then, the cat began to laugh.

Why are you laughing at me?

fond of …을 좋아하여	just then 바로 그 때
know 알다	begin(-began-begun) to
what 무엇	…하기 시작하다
be going to …할 것이다	laugh (소리내어)웃다
starve 굶어 죽다	why 어째서, 왜
surely 틀림없이, 꼭	laugh at 비웃다
die 죽다	

● ● ● ● ● ● ● ● ● ● ● ● ●

But, for the youngest son there was only the cat.
그러나 막내아들에게는 오직 고양이가 전부였습니다.

Well, I was just thinking that if you are hungry and worried about starving, why don't you cook me and eat me? You could use my fur to keep warm during the cold winter.

just 단지, 잠깐
think 생각하다
if 만약 …라면
hungry 배고픈
worry about …에 대해서 걱정하다
why don't you … 하는 게 어때요?
cook 요리하다

eat 먹다
use 사용하다
fur 털가죽
keep warm 따뜻하게 하다
during …동안[내내]
cold winter 추운 겨울

●●●●●●●●●●●●●●

why don't you cook me and eat me?
저를 요리해서 드시는 게 어떠세요?

You could use my fur to keep warm during the cold winter.
주인님은 추운 겨울 동안 따뜻하게 보내기 위해 저의 털을 사용할 수도 있어요.

I would never do that to you, Puss! Anyway, if you were not here, then I would be all alone. Then what would I do?

If you will buy me a brown bag and a pair of leather boots, you will see that I am worth more than a mill or an old donkey.

A brown bag and leather boots? How will that ever help me?

would (will의 과거형) …일 것이다	old donkey 늙은 당나귀
never 결코 … 않다	brown bag 갈색 가방
puss (부를 때)고양아	a pair of 한 켤레의
anyway 아무래도, 어쨌든	leather boots 가죽 장화
all alone 혼자서, 혼자 힘으로	see 알다[깨닫다]
worth 가치가 있는	ever 도대체, 대관절
mill 방앗간	help 도움이 되다

Anyway, if you were not here, then I would be all alone.
어쨌든 네가 여기 없었더라면 완전히 나 혼자 남겨졌을 거야.

you will see that I am worth more than a mill or an old donkey.
주인님은 제가 방앗간이나 늙은 당나귀보다 가치가 있다는 것을 깨닫게
되실 거예요.

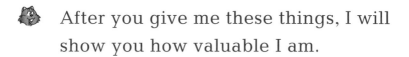 After you give me these things, I will show you how valuable I am.

You are a crazy cat, but, you never know. Why not?

So, the youngest son made up his mind to give the cat a chance.

after …한 뒤[다음]에
these things 이러한 것들
show 보여 주다
valuable 가치 있는
crazy 미친, 제정신이 아닌

youngest son 막내 아들
make up one's mind
    …하기로 마음먹다
give a chance 기회를 주다

● ● ● ● ● ● ● ● ● ● ● ● ●

After you give these things, I will show you how valuable I am.
주인님이 제게 가방과 장화를 주신 다음에 제가 얼마나 가치있는지를
보여 드릴게요.

So, the youngest son made up his mind to give the cat a chance.
그래서 막내 아들은 고양이에게 기회를 주기로 마음먹었습니다.

The cat looked so amazing in his new leather boots that the young master decided he must also buy him a hat and a cape as well.

I can not call you just plain Puss any more. From now on, you will be Puss-in-boots.

And I have a new name for you too, young master. From now on, you will be the Marquis of Carabas because I have great plans for you.

look 보이다	call 부르다
so ~ that … 너무 ~해서 …하다	plain 평범한
amazing 놀랄 만한, 굉장한	any more 더 이상
young master 젊은 주인	from now on 이제부터는
decide 결심하다	new name 새로운 이름
must …해야만 한다	Marquis of Carabas
buy 사다	카라바스 후작
hat 모자	because …때문에
cape 망토	great plan 멋진 계획
as well 게다가, 그 위에	

●●●●●●●●●●●●●

The cat looked so amazing in his new leather boots that the young master decided that he must buy him a hat and cape as well.
고양이가 새 가죽 장화를 신은 모습이 너무나 신기해 보여서 젊은 주인은 고양이에게 모자와 망토도 사 주어야겠다고 결심했습니다.

I can not call you just plain Puss any more. From now on, you will be Puss-in-boots. 나는 이제 더 이상 너를 단순히 평범한 고양이라고 부를 수 없어. 이제부터 너는 장화신은 고양이야.

I True or False

1. The miller owned many things.
2. The youngest son thought he was going to starve.
3. The cat told the miller's son to cook the donkey.
4. The miller's son did not buy the cat anything.
5. The miller's son decided to call the cat Puss-in-boots.

II Multiple Choice

1. Who was the strongest son?
   a. The oldest son was the strongest.
   b. The second son was the strongest.
   c. The youngest son was the strongest.

2. Who was the smartest son?
   a. The oldest son was the smartest.
   b. The second son was the smartest.
   c. The youngest son was the smartest.

정답은 p.94에

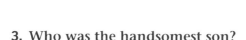

3. Who was the handsomest son?

   a. The oldest son was the handsomest.

   b. The second son was the handsomest.

   c. The youngest son was the handsomest.

4. What did the cat want the miller's son to buy for him?

   a. He wanted a mill and a donkey.

   b. He wanted a hat and a cape.

   c. He wanted a bag and a pair of leather boots.

5. What name did the cat give to the miller's son?

   a. The Marquis of Carabas

   b. The Duke of York

   c. Minsu

III **Fill in the Blanks - use the words in the word bank**
(each word is used once)

carry	chance	cold	fur	laugh
made	market	mill	then	worth

1. He could _____ bags of meal to the _____ with his donkey.

2. Just _____, the cat began to _____.

3. You could use my _____ to keep warm during the _____ winter.

4. You will see that I am _____ more than a _____ or an old donkey.

5. So the youngest son _____ up his mind to give the cat a _____.

정답은 p.94에

IV **Draw a line to connect the first half of each sentence with the second half:**

A   **B**

The poor miller •   • got his father's mill.

The miller's cat •   • had three sons.

The miller's •   • got his father's cat.
oldest son

The miller's •   • caught mice.
second son

The miller's •   • got his father's
youngest son   donkey.

SH-07-C
MP3

Chapter 2

So that night, Puss-in-boots went into the open field to begin working on his great plans. He started by filling his bag with a little delicious bran and sow thistle to attract young rabbits. He left his bag in the middle of the field and pretended to be dead. After a while, a family of young rabbits came hopping by, too young and inexperienced to understand the ways of the world.

that night 그 날 밤
go(-went-gone) into …로 가다
open field 드넓은 들판
begin 시작하다
fill with …을 가득 채우다
start 시작하다
a little 약간의, 조금의
delicious 맛있는
bran 왕겨
sow thistle 방가지똥(식물)
attract 끌다, 끌어당기다

in the middle of … 의 한가운데
pretend … 인 체하다
after a while 잠시 후에
a family of … 의 한 무리
rabbit 토끼
come(-came-come) by
    …에 다가가다
hop 뛰다
inexperienced 미숙한, 경험 없는
understand 알다, 이해하다

● ● ● ● ● ● ● ● ● ● ● ● ● ●

He started by filling his bag with a little delicious bran and sow thistle to attract young rabbits. 장화신은 고양이는 어린 토끼들을 끌어들이기 위하여 자루에 약간의 맛있는 왕겨와 방가지똥을 채워 넣기 시작했습니다.

After a while, a family of young rabbits came hopping by, too young and inexperienced to understand the ways of the world. 잠시 후에 세상을 이해하기에는 너무 어리고 미숙한 한 무리의 토끼들이 뛰면서 다가왔습니다.

One of the bunnies noticed the smell of
the cat's sack and decided to find out
what was inside. Without thinking,
he jumped into the open bag.

 Ah ha! You will make a delicious meal
for the King.

bunnies (bunny의 복수형)토끼들	without thinking 생각없이
notice 알아차리다, 깨닫다	jump into 뛰어들어가다
smell 냄새	open bag 열려진 가방
sack 자루	make …이 되다
decide to …하기로 결정하다	delicious 맛있는
find out 발견하다, 찾아 내다	meal 식사
inside 안쪽에	king 왕

● ● ● ● ● ● ● ● ● ● ● ● ●

Ah ha! You will make a delicious meal for the King!
아하, 이제 넌 왕께서 드실 맛있은 요리감이 될 거야!

With the rabbit in his bag,
Puss-in-boots began walking to the
King's castle. Before long, he stood
before the King of the land.

 Sir, I have a delicious rabbit here for
you. It is a gift from the noble lord, the
Marquis of Carabas.

 Please thank your master for his
kindness.

●●●●●●●●●●●●●

Before long, Puss-in-boots stood before the King of the land.
머지않아 장화신은 고양이는 그 나라의 왕 앞에 섰습니다.

Please thank your master for his kindness.
네 주인님께 호의에 감사드린다고 전하거라.

rabbit 토끼
bag 가방
begin(-began-begun) 시작하다
walk 걷다
castle 성
before long 머지않아, 곧
stand(-stood-stood) 서다
before …의 앞에

sir (손윗사람을 부를 때)폐하
here 여기에, 이곳에
gift 선물
noble 고귀한
lord (귀족의 명칭)…경
thank for …에 대해 감사하다
master 주인
kindness 친절, 호의

The next day, Puss-in-boots went hunting, and this time he was able to catch a large, plump partridge.
Once again, Puss-in-boots took his catch to the King of the land.

 My, my! Another gift from the Marquis of Carabas?

 My Master knows how much you enjoy a fine meal. He only wants to please and serve you.

 Here, I will show your master that I am grateful. Please take this bag to him as a gift from the King.

●●●●●●●●●●●●●

My Master knows how much you enjoy a fine meal.
저의 주인님은 폐하께서 얼마나 좋은 음식을 즐기시는지를 잘 알고 계십니다.

Please take this bag to him as a gift from the King.
이 가방을 왕으로부터의 선물로서 그에게 가져가도록 하여라.

next day 다음 날
go(-went-gone) hunting
  사냥하러 가다
this time 이번에는
be able to …할 수 있다
catch 잡다
large 커다란
plump 통통한, 살찐
partridge 메추라기
once again 다시 한 번
another 또 다른

know 알다
how much 얼마나 많이
enjoy 즐기다
fine meal 좋은 음식
only 그저, 단지
want to …하고 싶다
please 기쁘게 하다
serve 대접하다, 봉사하다
grateful 감사하는, 고마워하는
take 가져가다

As time went by, the cat gave more and more gifts to the King, and the King gave many gifts to the Marquis of Carabas. Soon the cat and the King became very good friends.

as time goes by 시간이
  지나감에 따라
give (-gave-given) 주다
more and more 더욱 더 많은
gift 선물

many 많은
soon 곧
become (-became-become)
  …이 되다
friend 친구

● ● ● ● ● ● ● ● ● ● ● ● ●

Soon, the cat and the King became very good friends.
고양이와 왕은 금새 아주 좋은 친구가 되었습니다.

Comprehension

I True or False

1. The rabbits were inexperienced.
2. Puss-in-boots stood before the King.
3. Puss-in-boots caught a big fish.
4. The King did not thank the Marquis of Carabas.
5. The king liked Puss-in-boots.

II Multiple Choice

1. **What did Puss-in-boots put in his bag to attract rabbits?**

   a. He put in grass and flowers.

   b. He put in bran and sow thistle.

   c. He put in carrots and cabbage.

2. **Why did Puss-in-boots pretend to be dead?**

   a. To get some sleep

   b. To catch a rabbit

   c. To trick his master

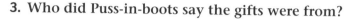

정답은 p.95에

3. Who did Puss-in-boots say the gifts were from?

   a. He said they were from Puss-in-boots.

   b. He said they were from the miller's son.

   c. He said they were from the Marquis of Carabas.

4. What did Puss-in-boots catch when he went hunting?

   a. He caught a partridge.

   b. He caught a fish.

   c. He caught a rabbit.

5. Why did the King give a bag to Puss-in-boots?

   a. To show that he was angry

   b. To show that he was rich

   c. To show that he was grateful

Comprehension

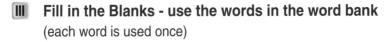

Checkup II

III **Fill in the Blanks - use the words in the word bank**
(each word is used once)

castle	field	fine	much	open
plans	thinking	walking	while	young

1. Puss-in-boots went into the open _____ to begin working on his great _____.

2. After a _____, a family of _____ rabbits came hopping by.

3. Without _____, he jumped into the _____ bag.

4. Puss-in-boots began _____ to the King's _____.

5. My Master knows how _____ you enjoy a _____ meal.

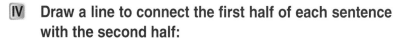

정답은 p.95에

IV **Draw a line to connect the first half of each sentence with the second half:**

A	**B**
One of the bunnies •	• wants to please and serve the King.
Puss-in-boots •	• was large and plump.
The partridge •	• was a good hunter.
The Marquis of Carabas •	• gave many gifts to the Marquis.
The King of the land •	• noticed the smell of the cat's sack.

Chapter 3

Then one day, Puss-in-boots decided it was time for his master to meet the King's daughter. She was the most beautiful princess in the entire world. He found out that the King would be taking his daughter for a carriage ride the very next day on the road by the river. He had no time to waste. Puss-in-boots ran back to come up with a plan.

● ● ● ● ● ● ● ● ● ● ● ●

He found out that the King would be taking his daughter for a carriage ride the very next day on the road by the river. 고양이는 왕이 바로 다음날 딸을 마차에 태우고 강 옆길을 지나간다는 사실을 알아냈습니다.

one day 어느 날
decide 결정하다, 결심하다
meet 만나다
daughter 딸
the most 가장 …한
beautiful 아름다운
princess 공주
in the entire world 온 세상에서
find(-found-found) out
  …을 알아내다

carriage 마차
ride 타다
the very next day 바로 다음 날
road 길, 도로
by the river 강 옆을, 강을 지나서
waste 낭비하다
run(-ran-run) back to
  …로 다시 달려가다
come up with a plan
  계획을 세우다[짜다]

Early the next morning,

Hurry Master. You must come with me and bathe in the river by the road.

What? Why should I bathe in the river?

Just do as I tell you and you will be very lucky! Take off your clothes and get into the water quickly.

But it's cold, and I don't know how to swim.

Trust me.

So, the youngest son did as the cat said.

Now, I have to hide these clothes and hope he will never have to wear them again.

Puss! Puss! Where are my clothes?

early the next morning	get into the water
다음 날 아침 일찍	물 속으로 들어가다
hurry 서두르다	quickly 재빨리
bathe 목욕하다	how to swim 수영하는 방법
tell 말하다	trust 신뢰하다, 믿다
lucky 운이 좋은, 행운인	say(-said-said) 말하다
take off (옷을)벗다	hide 숨기다, 숨다
clothes 옷, 의류	wear (옷 등을)입다

● ● ● ● ● ● ● ● ● ● ● ● ●

Just do as I tell you and you will be very lucky!
그냥 제 말대로 하세요, 그러면 주인님께 아주 좋은 일이 생길 거예요.

Now, I have to hide these clothes and hope he will never wear them again! 이제 난 이 옷들을 숨겨야겠다. 그리고 주인님이 다시는 이 옷들을 입지 않기를 바래.

Just then, the King's carriage came into view.

 Puss! Puss! My clothes!

Be quiet, or you will ruin everything! Listen to what I say. I will do all the talking, okay?

Help! My Lord, the Marquis of Carabas, is drowning!

carriage 마차
come(-came-come) into view
　시야에 들어오다
Be quiet 조용히 해라
ruin 망치다, 그르치다

listen to …을 듣다
what I say 내가 말하는 것
all the talking 모든 이야기
drown 물에 빠지다, 익사하다

● ● ● ● ● ● ● ● ● ● ● ● ●

Be quiet, or you will ruin everything!
조용히 하세요, 그렇지 않으면 모든 일을 망치고 말아요.

Guards! Hurry! Help that man!
My generous friend, the Marquis of
Carabas, must not drown!

So the guards of the King ran to the
rescue of the poor miller's son and
saved him just in time.

 Bring a robe to cover the Marquis!
He is shivering with a cold.

hurry 서두르다	miller's son 방앗간 주인의 아들
guard 친위병, 경비병	save 구하다, 모면하다
that man 저 남자	in time 때 맞추어, 늦지 않게
generous 인심 좋은, 관대한	bring 가져오다
run (-ran-run) to …로 달려가다	robe 예복, 길고 헐렁한 옷
rescue 구조, 구출	cover 덮어 주다, 감싸다
poor 가난한, 불쌍한	shiver with cold 추위로 덜덜 떨다

●●●●●●●●●●●●●

My generous friend, the Marquis of Carabas, must not drown.
내 관대한 친구인 카라바스 후작을 물에 빠져 죽게 해서는 안 된다!

Bring a robe to cover the Marquis!
후작의 몸을 덮어 줄 예복을 가져 오너라!

What has happened to the Marquis, and where are his clothes?

 A terrible thing has happened, Your Majesty. His clothes have all been stolen. We were riding along the riverside so peacefully, when suddenly a band of villains with weapons jumped out at us from behind some rocks and attacked us. The thieves stole everything he had and would have killed him too, but fortunately the Marquis escaped and jumped into the river. Unfortunately though, my master doesn't know how to swim.

• • • • • • • • • • • • •

What has happened to Marquis, and where are his clothes?
후작에게 무슨 일이 일어났느냐? 그리고 그의 옷은 어디에 있고?

His clothes have all been stolen. 후작님의 옷은 모두 도둑맞았습니다.

A band of villains with weapons jumped out at us from behind some rocks and attacked us. 무장한 한 무리의 악당들이 바위 뒤쪽에서 뛰쳐나와 저희를 공격했습니다.

happen 일어나다, 발생하다
terrible 끔찍한, 지독한
Your Majesty 폐하
steal(-stole-stolen) 훔치다
riverside along 강변을 따라서
peacefully 평화로이
suddenly 갑자기, 느닷없이
a band of 한 무리의
villain 악당, 악한
weapons 무기
jump at 갑자기 덮치다, 덤벼들다

from behind 뒤쪽에서
rock 바위
attack 습격하다, 공격하다
thieves (thief의 복수형)도둑들
kill 죽이다
fortunately 다행히도
unfortunately 불행히도
escape 도망치다
jump into …속으로 뛰어들다
though 그렇지만, 그러나

When the miller's son heard puss' clever story, he thought to himself.

 Hmm. My puss is very smart. He might really make me a rich man.

Puss was very happy and pleased when he saw the young princess admiring the miller's son.

clever 영리한
think(-thought-thought) to oneself
　혼잣말하다
smart 똑똑한
really 정말로

happy 행복한, 즐거운
see(-saw-seen) 보다
admire 감탄하다, 탐복하며
　바라보다

●●●●●●●●●●●●●

He might really make me a rich man.
고양이가 정말로 날 부자로 만들어 줄지도 모르겠군.

Puss was very happy and pleased when he saw the young princess
admiring the miller's son. 고양이는 젊은 공주가 방앗간 아들을 황홀하게
바라보는 모습을 보고는 매우 행복하고 즐거웠습니다.

The King sent his servants immediately back to the palace to order the master of the royal wardrobe to prepare clothing for the Marquis.

 Your Majesty, you are really too kind.

 Look at all the fine things the Marquis has given me. This is the least that I can do to repay him.

send(-sent-sent) 보내다
servant 부하, 신하
immediately 즉시, 당장
palace 궁전
order 주문하다, 명령하다
royal 왕실
wardrobe (왕실의)의상 관리인

prepare 준비하다
clothing 의류, 옷(=clothes)
kind 친절한, 상냥한
look at ⋯을 보다
fine 멋진, 훌륭한
least 최소한의 것, 보잘 것 없는 것
repay 보답하다, 돌려주다

● ● ● ● ● ● ● ● ● ● ● ● ● ●

Look at all the fine things the Marquis has given me.
후작이 짐에게 준 이 모든 훌륭한 물건들을 보게.

This is the least that I can do to repay him.
이것은 그에 대한 보답으로 내가 할 수 있는 최소한의 것이야.

In the King's fine clothes, the miller's youngest son looked like a fine noble, indeed. The King never doubted for a moment that the young man was a noble or a prince.

My friend, I am so glad that I finally met you! Since you don't have your own horse, will you please ride with us?

Your Majesty, it would be my pleasure.

clothes 옷	finally 마침내, 드디어
look like …처럼 보이다	meet(-met-met) 만나다
noble 귀족	since …이기 때문에, …이므로
indeed 정말, 참으로	own 자기 자신의
doubt 의심하다	horse 말
for a moment 잠시 동안, 한 순간	ride 타다
young man 젊은이	pleasure 즐거움, 기쁨

●●●●●●●●●●●●●●

In the King's fine clothes, the miller's youngest son looked like a fine noble, indeed.   방앗간 주인의 막내 아들은 왕의 멋진 옷을 입고 있으니 정말 훌륭한 귀족처럼 보였습니다.

Since you don't have your own horse, will you please ride with us? 자네에겐 말이 없으니 우리와 함께 타고 가겠나?

Your Majesty, it would be my pleasure.   영광이옵니다, 폐하.

Puss raced ahead of the carriage. He thought to himself.

I have given my master his name, and the King has given him his clothes. Now all he needs is land and a castle. The rich farmland and the castle belong to a wicked magician but I will claim it for my prince today.

race 달리다, 경주하다
ahead of …를 앞질러
think(-thought-thought) 생각하다
now 이제
need 필요한 것
land 땅, 나라
castle 성

rich 비옥한, 부유한
farmland 농지
belong to …에 속하다
wicked 사악한, 못된
magician 마법사
claim 획득하다, 요구하다
today 오늘

● ● ● ● ● ● ● ● ● ● ● ● ●

Puss raced ahead of the carriage.
고양이는 마차를 앞질러서 달려갔습니다.

Now all he needs is his land and a castle.
이제 주인님께 필요한 것은 땅과 성뿐이야.

I will claim it for my prince today.
나는 오늘 그 농지와 성을 우리 왕자님을 위해 빼앗을 거야.

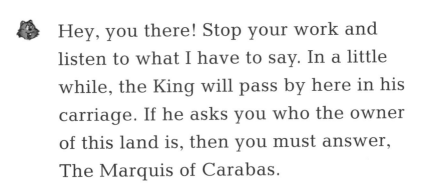 Hey, you there! Stop your work and listen to what I have to say. In a little while, the King will pass by here in his carriage. If he asks you who the owner of this land is, then you must answer, The Marquis of Carabas.

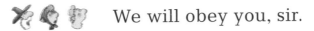 The Marquis of Carabas? Who is that?

If you obey me you will be very lucky!

 We will obey you, sir.

hey (시선을 끌 때)이봐, 잠깐
you there 여보시오, 이봐요
stop 멈추다, 정지하다
work 일, 작업
listen to …을 듣다
what I have to say
　　내가 말해야 하는 것
in a little while 잠시 후에
pass by 지나가다
here 이곳

carriage 마차
ask 묻다, 부탁하다
who 누구
owner 소유자, 주인
this land 이 땅
must …해야만 한다
answer 대답하다
obey 복종하다, 따르다
lucky 운이 좋은, 행운인
sir 나리, 선생님

In a little while, the King will pass by here in his carriage.
잠시 후에 왕이 마차를 타고 이곳을 지나갈 것입니다.

If you obey me you will be very lucky.
여러분이 제 말을 따라주신다면 큰 행운을 얻게 될 것입니다.

As the royal carriage came nearer to the field with the farmers, Puss-in-boots jumped aboard.

 Puss, I say, who owns this fine land?

 Just ask the farmers over there, sir.

 Good people, please tell me who owns this great land.

 This land belongs to the Marquis of Carabas, Your Majesty.

●●●●●●●●●●●●●

As the royal carriage came nearer to the field with the farmers, Puss-in-Boots jumped aboard. 왕실 마차가 농부들이 일하고 있는 밭으로 다가오자, 장화신은 고양이는 마차에 뛰어 올라탔습니다.

Puss, I say, who owns this fine land?
이보게 고양이, 이 비옥한 땅의 주인은 누구인가?

as …때(에)

royal carriage 왕실마차

come(-came-come) 오다

nearer (near의 비교급) 더 가까이

field 밭, 들판

farmer 농부

jump aboard 뛰어 올라타다

own 소유하다

just 단지, 그저

ask 묻다, 부탁하다

over there 저기에

good people 선량한 백성

tell 말하다

great 훌륭한, 멋진

belong to …에 속하다

Your Majesty 폐하

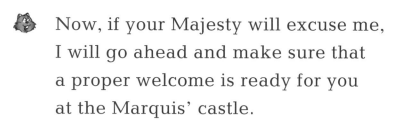 Now, if your Majesty will excuse me, I will go ahead and make sure that a proper welcome is ready for you at the Marquis' castle.

Castle? What castle?

Shhhhhh! Wait and see. Just trust me.

excuse 실례하다, 용서하다
go ahead 먼저 가다
make sure 확인하다
proper 적절한, 올바른
welcome 환영, 대접

ready for 준비가 된
shh (조용히 하라는 소리)쉬
wait 기다리다
trust 믿다, 신용하다

Now, if Your Majesty will excuse me, I will go ahead and make sure
that a proper welcome is ready for you at the Marquis castle.
이제, 만약 폐하만 괜찮으시다면, 저는 먼저 후작님의 성으로 가서 적절한
환영 준비가 되어 있는지 확인해 보겠습니다.

Comprehension

Checkup III

I True or False

1. Puss-in-boots wanted his master to meet the princess.

2. The miller's son knew how to swim.

3. Puss-in-boots said that a wicked magician stole his master's clothes.

4. The King wanted to repay the Marquis.

5. The farmers obeyed Puss-in-boots.

II Multiple Choice

1. Where did the King take his daughter for a carriage ride?

   a. They would go the very next day.

   b. They would go on the road by the river.

   c. They would go by the old mill.

2. What did Puss-in-boots tell his master to do?

   a. He told him to bathe in the river.

   b. He told him to hide his clothes.

   c. He told him to build a carriage.

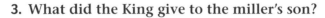

3. What did the King give to the miller's son?

   a. He gave him a horse.

   b. He gave him some clothes.

   c. He gave him a castle.

4. What did the son think about Puss-in-boots?

   a. He thought the cat was very handsome.

   b. He thought the cat was very strong.

   c. He thought the cat was very smart.

5. What did the King think about the miller's son?

   a. He thought he was a noble.

   b. He thought he was a magician.

   c. He thought he was a miller's son.

Comprehension

Checkup III

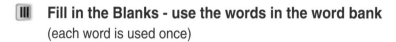

III **Fill in the Blanks - use the words in the word bank**
(each word is used once)

beautiful	castle	entire	friend	glad
great	little	needs	pass	tell

1. She was the most _____ princess in the _____ world.

2. My _____, I am so _____ that I finally met you.

3. Now all he _____ is land and a _____.

4. In a _____ while, the King will _____ by here in his carriage.

5. Good people, please _____ me who owns this _____ land.

IV **Draw a line to connect the first half of each sentence with the second half:**

A	B
Puss-in-boots •	• owned rich farmland and a castle.
The water in the river •	• admired the miller's son.
The King's guards •	• came up with a plan.
The young princess •	• saved the miller's son.
A wicked magician •	• was cold.

SH-07-C
MP3

Chapter 4

Once again, Puss raced ahead of the carriage. When he arrived at the wicked magician's castle, he paused for a moment to come up with a plan. Puss-in-boots was sure no one would lower the castle gate for a cat, but they would for a damsel in distress.

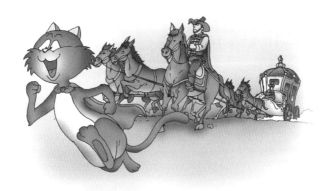

carriage 마차
arrive at …에 도착하다
wicked magician 사악한 마법사
pause 잠시 멈추다
for a moment 잠시 동안
come up with a plan
　　계획을 세우다[짜다]

sure 확신하는
no one 아무도 …이 아니다
lower 내리다
gate 문, 성문
damsel 소녀, 계집아이
in distress 곤궁에 처한

● ● ● ● ● ● ● ● ● ● ● ● ● ●

When he arrived at the wicked magician's castle, he paused for
a moment to come up with a plan.　고양이는 사악한 마법사의
성에 도착하자, 계획을 세우기 위하여 잠시 동안 멈춰 섰습니다.

Puss-in-Boots was sure no one would lower the castle gate for
a cat.　장화신은 고양이는 아무도 고양이를 위해서 성문을 내려주지는
않을 것이라고 확신했습니다.

Please, oh please, help me!
I am a damsel in distress and
I need your help!

When the large gate was lowered,
no one could see a damsel in distress
anywhere, so it was slowly raised
again.

When the large gate was lowered, no one could see a damsel in distress anywhere, so it was slowly raised again. 큰 성문이 내려졌을 때, 어디에도 곤경에 처한 소녀를 볼 수 있는 사람은 없었습니다. 그리고 성문은 다시 천천히 올려졌습니다.

● ● ● ● ● ● ● ● ● ● ● ● ●

please 제발, 부디   see(-saw-seen) 보다
help 돕다   anywhere 아무 데도
large 큰   slowly 천천히, 느리게
gate 문, 성문   raise 올리다
no one 아무도 …없다   again 다시

Meanwhile, Puss-in-boots was able to enter the castle unnoticed. Once inside, he began looking for the wicked magician.

Ah ha! There he is! He is the man I must conquer for my master. He owns the castle and everything the Marquis will need.

meanwhile 그 동안에
be able to …할 수 있다
enter 들어가다
castle 성
unnoticed 남의 눈에 띄지 않는
once …하자마자
begin(-began-begun) 시작하다

look for …을 찾다
wicked magician 사악한 마법사
must 해야만 하다
conquer 정복하다, 공략하다
my master 주인님
own 소유하다
everything 모든 것

Once inside, he began looking for the wicked magician.
안으로 들어가자마자, 고양이는 사악한 마법사를 찾기 시작했습니다.

He owns the castle and everything the Marquis will need.
그는 성과 후작이 필요로 하는 모든 것을 소유하고 있어.

Your Excellency! Please excuse me, but I have traveled from very far away to see you. You are famous throughout the world.

Why would you come so far just to see me?

I heard that you were the greatest magician in the entire world. So, I wanted to see for myself if it was really true.

● ● ● ● ● ● ● ● ● ● ● ● ●

Your Excellency! Please excuse me, but I have traveled from very far away to see you.
존경하는 마법사님! 부디 저를 용서하세요. 그렇지만 저는 당신을 만나기 위해서 아주 먼 곳에서 왔습니다.

Why would you come so far just to see me?
그렇게 먼 곳에서 왜 나를 만나러 왔지?

So, I wanted to see for myself if it was really true.
그래서, 전 그것이 정말 사실이라면 제 자신을 위해서 보고 싶었습니다.

Your Excellency 존경하는 분
Please 제발, 부디
excuse 용서하다
travel 여행하다
from very far away 아주 먼
  곳으로부터
see(-saw-seen) 만나다, 보다
famous 유명한
throughout …의 전체에 걸쳐서

come(-came-come) 오다
hear(-heard-heard) 듣다
so far 그렇게 멀리서
entire world 전 세계
want 원하다
myself 나 자신
really 진심으로, 정말로
true 진실, 사실

Of course it is true! I can turn myself into anything! I can turn myself into a lion, a bear, an elephant or a tiger!

Impossible! I don't believe you can turn yourself into a lion.

of course 물론   elephant 코끼리
turn into …으로 변하다   tiger 호랑이
anything 무엇이든, 뭐든지 impossible 불가능한
lion 사자   believe 믿다
bear 곰   yourself 당신 자신

● ● ● ● ● ● ● ● ● ● ● ● ●

Of course it is true! I can turn myself into anything!
물론 사실이지! 나는 나 자신을 무엇으로든 변신시킬 수 있어.

Impossible! I don't believe you can turn yourself into a lion.
불가능해요! 나는 당신이 사자로 변할 수 있다고는 믿지 않아요.

Without any more words, the magician immediately turned himself into a huge, ferocious, and very scary lion. Puss was so scared that he begged the magician to turn himself back.

 Okay, I believe you now that you can turn yourself into large creatures. But, can you also turn yourself into small creatures, like a mouse or a rat? That must be too difficult even for someone like you.

without …없이
any more 더 이상의
words 말, 이야기
immediately 즉시, 당장
huge 거대한, 막대한
ferocious 사나운, 포악한
scary 무서운
scared 깜짝 놀란, 겁에 질린
beg 빌다, 청하다

Okay 좋은, 괜찮은
creature 생물
like …처럼
mouse 생쥐
rat 쥐
must be 틀림없이 …일 것이다
difficult 어려운
even 비록[가령] …이라도
someone 누군가, 어떤 사람

● ● ● ● ● ● ● ● ● ● ● ● ● ●

Without any more words, the magician immediately turned
himself into a huge, ferocious, and very scary lion.
더 이상의 말도 없이, 마법사는 즉시 거대하고, 사나운 그리고 무서운
사자로 변신했습니다.

That must be too difficult even for someone like you.
그건 설령 당신 같은 분이라 해도 너무 어려울 것임에 틀림없어요.

What do you mean too difficult? Watch what I can do!

In the blink of an eye, the wicked magician turned himself into a small mouse.

Ah ha, my friend! You may be the greatest magician in the entire world, but I am the greatest mouser!

Puss pounced on the mouse, and that was the end of the wicked magician.

what 무엇
mean 의미하다
in the blink of an eye
  눈 깜짝할 사이에
wicked 사악한
magician 마법사
turn into …으로 바꾸다

small 작은
friend 친구
may …일지도 모르다
entire world 온 세상
pounce 갑자기 덤벼들다
mouser 쥐를 잡는 동물
end 최후, 종말

Ah ha, my friend! You may be the greatest magician in the entire world, but I am the greatest moser! 아하, 나의 친구! 당신은 세상에서 가장 위대한 마법사일 거요. 그러나 난 쥐를 잡는 동물로서는 가장 위대하지.

Puss pounced on the mouse, and that was the end of the wicked magician. 고양이는 갑자기 쥐에게 덤벼들었습니다. 그리고 그것이 사악한 마법사의 최후였습니다.

Attention guards! Please prepare to welcome your new master, the Marquis of Carabas! He will be the new master of the castle!

All of the servants were so happy to hear the news of a new master, that they immediately obeyed Puss.

attention 주의, 주목
guard 경비병
prepare 준비하다
welcome 환영
new master 새로운 주인
castle 성

servant 하인
happy 행복한
hear(-heard-heard) 듣다
news 소식
immediately 즉시, 당장
obey 복종하다, 따르다

●●●●●●●●●●●●●

Please prepare to welcome your new master, the Marquis of
Carabas! 여러분의 새로운 주인이신 카라바스 후작님의 환영 준비를
하도록 하시오!

All of the servants were so happy to hear the news of an new
master, that they immediately obey puss. 모든 하인들은 새로운
주인에 대한 소식을 듣고 매우 기뻐하며 즉시 고양이의 말에 따랐습니다.

Just then, the royal carriage arrived. Bowing low, Puss said.

 Welcome, your Majesty, to the home of my lord and master, the Marquis of Carabas.

Everyone was so happy with the new master, who was so young and handsome, that the finest feast ever was prepared and everyone had a wonderful time.

just then 바로 그 때
royal 왕실
carriage 마차
arrive 도착하다
bow 절하다
say(-said-said) 말하다
Your Majesty 폐하
lord 주인님, …경

everyone 모두, 모든 사람
young 젊은
handsome 잘생긴
old 늙은, 나이 먹은
finest 가장 훌륭한
feast 축연, 잔치
ever 이제까지
wonderful 훌륭한, 굉장한

● ● ● ● ● ● ● ● ● ● ● ● ●

Everyone was so happy with the new master, who was so young and handsome, that the finest feast ever was prepared and everyone had a wonderful time.   모든 사람들이 상당히 젊고 잘생긴 새로운 주인과 더불어 매우 기뻐하였습니다. 이전에 없던 가장 훌륭한 만찬이 준비되었고 모두가 즐거운 시간을 보냈습니다.

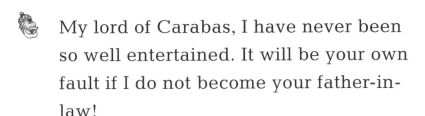 My lord of Carabas, I have never been so well entertained. It will be your own fault if I do not become your father-in-law!

Would you really be willing to marry me, princess?

I would love to marry you, Marquis of Carabas.

The next day, the poor miller's son and the most beautiful princess in the whole world were married. And, everyone lived happily ever after.

have never been 결코 …한
  적이 없다
well 잘
entertain 대접하다, 환대하다
own 자기 자신의
fault 실수
become …이 되다
father-in-law 장인, 시아버지

willing to (…하는 것을)꺼리지 않는
marry 결혼하다
princess 공주
poor 가난한
beautiful 아름다운
whole 전부의, 전체의
live 살다
ever after 그 후 내내

● ● ● ● ● ● ● ● ● ● ● ● ●

My lord of Carabas, I have never been so well entertained. It will
be your own fault if I do not become your father-in-law.
카라바스 경, 짐은 이처럼 훌륭한 접대를 받아본 적이 없소. 만일 짐이
카라바스경의 장인이 되지 못한다면 그것은 경의 실수일 것이오.

The next day, the poor miller's son and the most beautiful
princess in the whole world were married. 다음 날, 가난한 방앗간
집의 아들과 세상에서 가장 아름다운 공주는 결혼을 했습니다.

Comprehension

Checkup IV

I **True or False**

1. Puss-in-boots pretended to be a magician.

2. Puss-in-boots was scared of the lion.

3. Puss-in-boots said he was the greatest mouser in the world.

4. The servants did not want to obey Puss-in-boots.

5. The princess wanted to marry the miller's son.

II **Multiple Choice**

1. **Who saw Puss-in-boots enter the castle?**

   a. The guards saw him enter the castle.

   b. The wicked magician saw him enter the castle.

   c. No one saw him enter the castle.

2. **What magic could the wicked magician do?**

   a. He could turn into anything.

   b. He walk through the walls.

   c. He could see the future.

3. **Who killed the wicked magician?**

   a. The miller's son killed him.

   b. Puss-in-boots killed him.

   c. The servants killed him.

4. **What did the servants think of their new master?**

   a. They were happy.

   b. They were sad.

   c. They didn't care.

5. **Who was the new master of the castle?**

   a. Puss-in-boots was the new master.

   b. The Marquis of Carabas was the new master.

   c. The King was the new master.

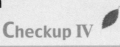

III **Fill in the Blanks - use the words in the word bank**
(each word is used once)

conquer	difficult	distress	like	lower
man	myself	see	sure	wanted

1. Puss-in-boots was _____ no one would _____ the castle gate for a cat.

2. No one could _____ a damsel in _____ anywhere.

3. He is the _____ I must _____ for my master.

4. So I _____ to see for _____ if it was really true.

5. That must be too _____ even for someone _____ you.

정답은 p.97에

IV Draw a line to connect the words that are opposites of each other:

A	**B**
Old •	• Cold
Warm •	• Raise
Poor •	• Wicked
Kind •	• Young
Lower •	• Rich

Checkup I (24~27p)

Ⅰ **1.** F **2.** T **3.** F **4.** F **5.** T

Ⅱ **1.** a **2.** b **3.** c **4.** c **5.** a

Ⅲ **1.** carry, market **2.** then, laugh
3. fur, cold **4.** worth, mill
5. made, chance

A		B
The poor miller	● ╲╱ ●	got his father's mill.
The miller's cat	● ╳ ●	had three sons.
The miller's oldest son	● ╳ ●	got his father's cat.
The miller's second son	● ╳ ●	caught mice.
The miller's youngest son	● ╱╲ ●	got his father's donkey.

Comprehension Checkup

Checkup II (38~41p)

I　**1.** T　　**2.** T　　**3.** F　　**4.** F　　**5.** T

II　**1.** b　　**2.** b　　**3.** c　　**4.** a　　**5.** c

III　**1.** field, plans　　**2.** while, young
　　3. thinking, open　　**4.** walking, castle
　　5. much, fine

　　　　　　　A　　　　　　　　　　　　**B**

IV　One of the bunnies　　　　　　wants to please and
　　　　　　　　　　　　　　　　　serve the King.

　　Puss-in-boots　　　　　　　　was large and plump.

　　The partridge　　　　　　　　was a good hunter.

　　The Marquis of　　　　　　　gave many gifts to the
　　Carabas　　　　　　　　　　　Marquis.

　　The King of　　　　　　　　　noticed the smell of the
　　the land　　　　　　　　　　　cat's sack.

Comprehension Checkup

Checkup III (66~69p)

| I | **1.** T | **2.** F | **3.** F | **4.** T | **5.** T |

| II | **1.** b | **2.** a | **3.** b | **4.** c | **5.** a |

III **1.** beautiful, entire   **2.** friend, glad
3. needs, castle   **4.** little, pass
5. tell, great

A B

IV Puss-in-boots   owned rich farmland
                         and a castle.

The water in   admired the miller's
the river   son.

The King's guards   came up with a plan.

The young princess   saved the miller's son.

A wicked magician   was cold.

Comprehension Checkup

Checkup IV (90~93p)

I   **1.** F   **2.** T   **3.** T   **4.** F   **5.** T

II   **1.** c   **2.** a   **3.** b   **4.** a   **5.** b

III   **1.** sure, lower   **2.** see, distress
       3. man, conquer   **4.** wanted, myself
       5. difficult, like

IV

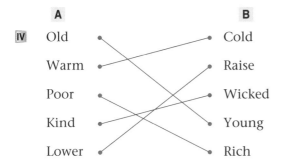

A	B
Old	Cold
Warm	Raise
Poor	Wicked
Kind	Young
Lower	Rich

Word List

다음은 이 책에 나오는 단어와 숙어를 수록한 것입니다.
＊표는 중학교 영어 교육 과정의 기본 어휘입니다.

C

Y

Notes

Story House
07. Puss in Boots 장화신은 고양이

펴낸이	임 병 업
펴낸곳	(주)월드컴 에듀
등록	2000년 1월 17일
주소	서울특별시 강남구 언주로 120
	인스토피아 빌딩 912호
전화	02)3273-4300(대표)
팩스	02)3273-4303
홈페이지	www.wcbooks.co.kr
이메일	wc4300@wcbooks.co.kr